The Adventures of Blaze Sharp

BOOK ONE

KING AUTHOR

Paperback ISBN 978-1-0689320-0-7

Ebook ISBN 978-1-0689320

Cover Art by Betty Martinez

CHAPTER ONE

Birth of Blaze Sharp

CHRISTINE HOLY MADE her way to the Christian Jesus Lord and Savior kindergarten class, striding confidently in a three-piece pride-striped pantsuit that matched her vibrant hair, dyed to echo the hues of the lesbian flag. Instead of the traditional nun's robes designated as her school uniform, she embraced her individuality with flair. Her mismatched eyes—one a fiery orange, the other a soft pink—reflected not only her unique appearance but also her rebellious spirit. Unyielding in her beliefs, Christine challenged the teachings of her school, driven by a profound sense of conviction.

Christine greeted each of the girls with a flirtatious smile. "Hello, Abigail, nice to see you again.

Beatrix, looking good. Claire, call me. Dianne, always a pleasure," she purred, her tone dripping with charm until she reached the last one. "Zelda Black, the best of the best," she said with extra flirtation, tossing a rose into the air for Zelda to catch. "You are as beautiful as any flower. Unfortunately, my classroom awaits, though it pains me to leave your company," Christine remarked haughtily, her confidence unwavering.

"Your class started forty minutes ago," Zelda replied matter-of-factly.

Christine's smirk faltered for a moment before she shrugged it off. "Then I guess I'll be early today," she retorted sarcastically, dismissing the notion with a flick of her hand.

Christine entered the classroom with an air of nonchalance. "I'm here," she announced, disregarding the fact that she was late.

"You're late again, Miss Holy," scolded Ms. Mariam, the teacher.

Ignoring the reprimand, Ms. Mariam instructed the class, "Recite the rule of marriage." "Marriage is between a man and a woman," chorused every student except for Christine. "Miss Holy, you did not recite the rule of marriage," admonished Ms. Mariam.

"I did not recite it because I do not believe in it," Christine retorted sharply, sparking an argument between her and Ms. Mariam that culminated in Christine being sent to Principal Aaron's office.

Later that day, Christine's mother, Josephine, was forced to pick her up from school early. "Christine, you'll never find a husband if you keep behaving like this," Josephine scolded angrily.

"Fine by me, I don't want one," Christine snapped in anger.

The next day, Christine would utter words to her parents that would change all their lives forever. They just didn't know it at the time.

The next day, in the Holy residence, Christine gathered all her courage. "Mother, Father, I have something I need to tell you," she said, her voice steady but her heart pounding.

"What is it, Christine?" her father, Marik, asked, his brow furrowing with concern.

"Are you finally done with this rebellious phase of yours? Have you decided to be a good girl and be saved by Christian Jesus?" her mother, Josephine, interjected, her tone hopeful.

"The opposite, actually," Christine replied, drawing upon every ounce of strength she could muster. "Mother, Father, it's about time that you knew… I'm gay," she declared, bracing herself for their reaction.

Her parents' expressions turned from curiosity to shock and horror as the weight of Christine's words sank in.

"Nonsense! The Holy family always enters the kingdom of heaven," Marik scolded, his voice firm with conviction.

"We will not allow you to be dragged down to the underworld. Even if we must convert you by force!" Josephine declared in frustration, her tone tinged with desperation.

"You can try, but you'll never succeed!" Christine countered defiantly, her confidence unwavering in the face of her parents' resolve.

At that point, Christine was subjected to a series of twelve conversion therapy camps, each more brutal than the last. In the first camp, she endured punishment on the Catherine wheel. By the fifth camp, she was subjected to crucifixion, electrocution, and having her head trapped in a vice with holes drilled into it, all simultaneously. The twelfth camp was the most horrifying of all, where she was confined to a tower engulfed in flames, enduring temperatures reaching unimaginable levels for ten relentless days and nights. Despite enduring such excruciating agony, Christine remained resolute in her refusal to convert.

Christine remained steadfast as the only one who resisted conversion. While some proved more resilient than others—Zelda Black endured five conversion camps before conforming—nothing could alter Christine's true self. However, her refusal to be swayed caught the attention of a particular group who saw her as a valuable asset to their cause.

Josephine enrolled Christine in Saint Joan's Girls Academy of Atrociously Rebellious Chaos, convinced that it would ensure Christine's salvation. Little did she know, the academy had its own agenda, and the true nature of Saint Joan was far from what it seemed.

Saint Joan led Christine to a clandestine facility bustling with girls training to become detectives, spies, mercenaries, and assassins. Each one sported pride-striped outfits, mostly suits, and hair dyed in the colors of the lesbian flag.

"Welcome to the lesbian branch of the Lethal Government Battle Tactics agency. I am your new leader, Sorceress Fiend," Saint Joan, now revealed as Sorceress Fiend, introduced.

"You want me to become an LGBT assassin

spymaster?" Christine inquired, a glimmer of hope in her voice.

"Yes, all you need now is a name. All our agents choose their own," Sorceress Fiend explained.

"I've just thought of the perfect one. From now on, I am known only as Blaze Sharp!" Christine declared confidently, adopting her new identity.

Love of Blaze Sharp

BLAZE SHARP dedicated years of rigorous training at the agency. Despite facing opponents twice her height, thrice her weight, and much older than her—given that she joined at the age of ten—who were also stronger, faster, and more experienced, she never faltered.

Instead, she worked tirelessly, surpassing all expectations to become the agency's top member.

Blaze Sharp's arsenal included a Remington 700 sniper rifle, a Sig Sauer MCX Rattler assault rifle, a Mac 10 sub machine gun, a Walther PPK pistol, a repeating pistol crossbow with flaming strychnine-tipped bolts, and an array of throwing combat knives with cyanide-coated blades capable of igniting with the flip of a switch. All the agency's bullets were crafted from Shamure, a material that completely dissolves upon contact with blood over time. Additionally, the arrows, throwing weapons, and melee weapons were forged from Pridium, a substance fifty times stronger than steel, three percent lighter than steel, impervious to melting, and capable of cutting through anything but itself.

Blaze Sharp ventured to a nearby gay bar, taking advantage of the agency's policy allowing underage members to enter as long as they abstained from alcohol. She hoped to meet a potential girlfriend or perhaps engage in a one-night stand. However, her expectations were soon overturned.

As the atmosphere in the bar grew tense, it became evident that it was about to be robbed by members of the Corrupt Homicidal Undercover Rascals Causing Havoc, better known as CHURCH. One of the assailants pressed a double-barrel shotgun against Blaze Sharp's ribcage, demanding her wallet.

"I have four dollars in my wallet, and that's for my last drink!" Blaze announced defiantly, refusing to comply with the robber's demands. CHURCH was the agency's sworn enemy, and Blaze was determined not to let them succeed in their criminal activities.

In a split-second decision, as the robber prepared to pull the trigger, Blaze swiftly disarmed him, seizing control of the situation and turning the tables by using the robber's own weapon against him.

As chaos erupted in the bar, other members of CHURCH began hurling drinking glasses at Blaze Sharp. Amidst the turmoil, the bartender tossed a duffel bag filled with assorted melee weapons into the fray. The robbers wasted no time grabbing weapons and launching attacks on Blaze.

She first faced off against a thug wielding a 2x4 with a handle. With quick reflexes, Blaze disarmed him and seized control of the makeshift weapon. Turning the tables, she skillfully wielded the 2x4 against her assailants, fighting back with determination. In the midst of the skirmish, one of the punks, overwhelmed by fear, made a hasty retreat.

Undeterred by the broken 2x4, Blaze Sharp continued to confront the thugs head-on. "Is that all you've got, you idiots?!" she bellowed, tossing aside the fractured weapon. In a sudden turn of events, she found herself hurled onto a table with bone-shattering force, causing it to splinter into pieces.

As another thug brandished a piece of rebar, attempting to strike her, Blaze swiftly intervened, tripping him and seizing the weapon for herself. With deft precision, she turned the tables, delivering blows to both him and another assailant with the rebar.

Just as she regained her footing, the cowardly punk who had fled earlier returned, wielding a STEN machine gun. Without hesitation, he opened fire on Blaze, but in a stroke of luck, a fallen thug rose to his feet, inadvertently intercepting the gunfire. Miraculously, Blaze emerged from the chaos unscathed.

Blaze Sharp hurled the rebar at the cowardly punk, delivering a fatal blow. Seizing the STEN gun, she unleashed a barrage of bullets, cutting down half of the thugs until the weapon emptied. With ruthless efficiency, she used the gun as a makeshift hammer, crushing the skull of one of the assailants.

Turning to face the remaining thugs, Blaze demonstrated her lethal prowess. She hurled the gun like a javelin, impaling another thug, before engaging in hand-to-hand combat with the rest. Disarming one assailant, she turned his own weapon against him, inflicting fatal wounds.

As another thug attacked with glass shards, Blaze swiftly turned the tables, using his own hand to deliver a fatal blow. When another attempted to strangle her, she resorted to biting his neck, severing his carotid arteries and causing him to bleed out.

In a final confrontation, Blaze disarmed the last thug, breaking his arm before delivering a fatal blow to the head. Exhausted from the intense battle, she made her way to the bar, pouring herself a glass of alcohol-free wine.

"Cheers," Blaze said wearily, raising her glass in a toast, the adrenaline of the fight beginning to ebb away.

"That was very brave, miss," the bartender said, attempting to discern Blaze's identity. "Sharp. Blaze Sharp," she replied, taking a sip of her wine before recognizing the bartender. "Zelda Black, is that you?" Blaze asked in surprise.

"That's right!" Zelda confirmed, pointing the double-barrel shotgun from earlier at Blaze's face.

"I thought you were behind this when you provided the robbers with weapons," Blaze remarked calmly, sipping her wine without a hint of fear.

"I had no choice. I owed money to the CHURCH, and they were supposed to collect it today. If they don't, they'll kill my cat!" Zelda explained desperately.

As Blaze glanced to her left, she noticed one last thug pointing a loaded Walther P38 pistol at Zelda Black's black cat.

"Your death will easily cover my debts, Blaze," Zelda said in a panic.

"Then pull the trigger. Left or right, I couldn't care less," Blaze retorted, finishing her glass of wine.

Zelda pulled the right trigger, but nothing happened. She then pulled the left trigger, with the same result.

"I shot that guy with both barrels at once," Blaze chuckled. "Then the cat dies," the thug threatened.

"Stop. I'll pay the debt," Blaze declared, searching through her clothes and retrieving her Walther PPK pistol. She aimed and fired, destroying the thug's weapon, then forced the silencer of her pistol into his eye and pulled the trigger, causing his head to explode.

"Here's your cat back," Blaze said, returning Zelda's pet. "How can I ever thank you?" Zelda asked.

"Forget everything you learned at the conversion camps, and we're even. Ciao," Blaze said, before leaving.

Blaze Sharp rode the bus home that night, enjoying the perk of free transportation courtesy of the agency. However, her journey was far from peaceful, reminiscent of the chaos at the bar less than an hour earlier. A gang of drunken CHURCH members crashed their car next to the bus, and despite Blaze's intuition telling her they were trouble, the bus driver allowed them aboard.

Sensing trouble brewing, Blaze motioned for the bus driver to exit the vehicle and leave their phone behind, knowing they wouldn't need it until she was finished teaching the unruly drunks some manners.

One of the drunks noticed Blaze Sharp still on the bus. 'Hey, what are you still doing here, hot stuff?' he slurred, clearly unaware he was barking up the wrong tree.

'You want to die?' Blaze retorted, unloading her pistol and placing the empty clip back in the gun before setting it down on the floor. The drunks erupted into hysterical laughter.

In a brazen act, one of them landed a punch on Blaze's face. Though she felt the sting, it was nothing compared to what they were about to face.

A massive fistfight erupted between Blaze Sharp and the drunks on the bus. One of them attempted to attack her with a rum bottle, but she swiftly caught it and smashed it against his head. As the brawl intensified, Blaze realized the drunks were tougher adversaries than she had anticipated. In desperation, she improvised weapons from her wristwatch and spare key. She mercilessly beat a guy's face in with the watch wrapped around her fist, then stabbed her spare key into another's ribcage, stomping it in further.

Despite their efforts to throw her out of the window, Blaze returned to the bus, unleashing a relentless assault with one of her knives, eviscerating the remaining drunks. As the last one attempted to reload her gun and shoot her, Blaze broke a pipe off the bus and used it to fatally injure him, crushing his arm and skull.

Once the chaos subsided, Blaze retrieved her gun and returned the phone to the driver. 'Sorry about the mess,' she said as she walked away, her home not far from the scene.

Back at the agency, Blaze Sharp received a mission directly from Prime Minister Pontius Pilates, the leader and founder of the organization. Her assignment: to protect Pontius' great-niece, Helen. Helen Pilates had recently come out as bisexual, and as a result, CHURCH had targeted her for elimination. Blaze Sharp was entrusted with Helen's safety, with her life on the line.

However, when Blaze first met Helen face-to-face, she experienced an emotion she had never felt before: true love.

"Who are you?" Helen questioned Blaze.

"I'm Agent Blaze Sharp of the Lethal Government Battle Tactics agency. I've been assigned to protect you," Blaze replied.

"You're my bodyguard? You're my age and not exactly what I picture when I think of an action hero. You seem more like a potential girlfriend than a guardian," Helen remarked, skeptical of Blaze's ability to protect her.

"There's no reason why I can't be both," Blaze responded, a hint of flirtation in her tone. "Are you hitting on me? If this is the caliber of the agency's agents, my great uncle will never

convince me to join," Helen judged, expressing her disdain for the agency and its operatives.

"I happen to be one of the finest agents the agency has," Blaze boasted confidently. "You, the best? Don't make me laugh," Helen scoffed dismissively.

Sensing imminent danger, Blaze sprang into action. "Watch out!" she shouted, pulling Helen out of harm's way just as an RPG-7 rocket exploded nearby. Swiftly, Blaze positioned herself and eliminated the assailant with precise sniper fire from her Remington 700 rifle.

Stunned by Blaze's display of heroism, Helen admitted, "You're tougher than you look, I'll give you that."

"Go, go, go. There's more where he came from around here," Blaze ordered with the fearless determination of a seasoned professional.

Blaze Sharp and Helen took cover behind a nearby wall, their hearts racing as they observed a squad of seven CHURCH soldiers approaching, one of them wielding a deadly flamethrower. Without hesitation, Blaze fired a crossbow bolt into the fuel tanks of the flamethrower, triggering a devastating explosion that engulfed the entire squad in a fiery inferno.

Gesturing for Helen to follow, Blaze prepared to move forward, but their path was quickly obstructed once again.

Blaze Sharp and Helen found themselves confronted by a gauntlet of armed CHURCH soldiers. Assessing the situation, Blaze addressed Helen. "So, what are we up against here? Six opponents, four armed with weapons: a dolabra pickaxe, a katana sword, a gladius sword, and a set of throwing tomahawks. Helen, start counting. This should take no more than twenty-three seconds," Blaze calculated, stating the facts plainly.

The first CHURCH soldier charged at them, attempting to start a fistfight with Blaze Sharp, but she swiftly blocked his punch with her poisoned knife, incapacitating him. As the next assailant lunged forward with a dolabra pickaxe, Blaze deftly ducked, slashing his stomach with lethal precision.

The following opponent rushed in with a gladius sword, but Blaze sidestepped the attack and swiftly slit his throat. Evading the next strike from a katana sword, Blaze seized the opportunity to stab the assailant in the back, neutralizing the threat.

When another enemy attempted a kick to her face, Blaze expertly blocked with her knife, the poisoned blade sealing his fate. As the last remaining opponent began hurling tomahawks at her, Blaze reacted swiftly, destroying them in mid-flight with her Sig Sauer MCX Rattler assault rifle, before unleashing a barrage of bullets upon him.

"How was that?" Blaze Sharp asked rhetorically, feeling confident in her abilities. However, as she turned around, she was horrified by what she saw behind her.

Before Blaze Sharp stood a CHURCH sergeant, holding Helen hostage at gunpoint with a loaded full-auto Mauser pistol pressed against her head.

"Let her go. Take me in her place," Blaze Sharp negotiated, her voice steady despite the tension in the air.

The sergeant, recognizing Blaze Sharp as a much bigger prize, agreed to the exchange, knowing that with her dead, their target would soon be caught and slaughtered. Blaze bravely swapped places with Helen, allowing herself to become the hostage.

"Helen, run!" she ordered, her voice urgent with

concern for her companion's safety. "Any last requests?" the CHURCH sergeant taunted.

"Yeah, just this!" Blaze Sharp snapped, swiftly stomping on the sergeant's foot, breaking his nose with a swift elbow strike, flipping him onto his back, and unleashing a barrage of bullets from her MAC 10 submachine gun.

The next day, Blaze Sharp would receive news from the prime minister that would change her life forever.

"With all due respect, I don't need a partner," Blaze Sharp asserted as Prime Minister Pontius assigned her a new partner.

"This agent only agreed to join if she could be your partner," Pontius ordered firmly.

"But, sir, I am the agency's best. If I were partnered with a rookie, she would just slow me down," Blaze debated.

"Trust me, it will be worth it," Pontius declared confidently.

"Can't you just partner her up with another member of the bisexual branch?" Blaze suggested.

"At least you should meet her before you say no," Pontius said, hinting at a surprise.

Entering the room was a young woman, the same age as Blaze Sharp. Her hair was dyed in the colors of the bisexual pride flag, one eye blue while the other was pink, and she wore a pride-striped outfit consisting of a jacket, shirt, and skirt. Blaze Sharp immediately recognized her.

"Helen?!" Blaze exclaimed with joy.

"I knew you would remember me. But I no longer go by Helen. From now on, my name is Silver Shadow!" Helen, now Silver Shadow, announced, introducing her new identity.

Blaze and Silver were thrilled to be working together again, their happiness evident as they shared a nonstop kiss for five minutes.

CHAPTER THREE

Partner of Blaze Sharp

AFTER WORKING TOGETHER and dating for several months, Blaze Sharp and Silver Shadow decided it was time to live together. They found the perfect house that met all their needs: located in an LGBT-friendly neighborhood, a new modern building with a built-in safe room, and most importantly, no religious establishments within sixty kilometers. Additionally, it had everything else they could need or want.

However, they encountered a trivial problem upon arrival. "Who in the world are you two ladies, and what are you doing in my house?" demanded the younger of the two owners, a father and son duo. Unfazed, Blaze and Silver dumped a duffel bag full of diamonds onto the table.

"We're buying this place!" Blaze declared firmly, refusing to accept no for an answer. "This is our offer. Take it and get out," Silver added, her tone laced with authority. "Not bad. You've got a deal," the father agreed.

"No, they don't. I get a say in this too!" the son interjected, only to be met with a punch from Blaze.

"We don't care! You both have until dawn to pack your stuff and get out of our house. And to ensure you finish on time, we'll even help you pack. The movers are already on their way," Blaze and Silver announced, leaving the owners with no choice but to comply.

Three weeks later, 'Silver, my love, something has been troubling me,' Blaze Sharp mentioned.

'What is it, darling Blaze?' Silver Shadow asked, concern in her voice.

'How did your parents react to you coming out of the closet?' Blaze inquired, seeking comfort from her beloved Silver.

'They were very supportive, dear Blaze. What about yours?' Silver replied, curious about Blaze's family.

'Silver, sweetheart, my parents still think I'm at some sort of conversion camp,' Blaze confessed, causing Silver's expression to shift to one of shock.

'How awful. Don't you think that if they met me-' Silver began, but Blaze cut her off, knowing where her thoughts were leading.

'They would have hired an exorcist or something like that. They're not nearly as progressive as the agency. I fear they still believe every lie that CHURCH spreads throughout the world,' Blaze explained before Silver could finish her sentence.

'I see. Well then, would you at least like to meet my parents?' Silver asked, offering her support.

'Sure thing, my love. It would be nice to meet a family where I can truly be myself,' Blaze agreed.

'One thing first: they don't know about the agency, so we'll need to use our given names and birth surnames in front of them. Which reminds me, you never told me yours,' Silver pointed out.

'Christine Holy,' Blaze said, feeling a pang of discomfort at the mention of her birth name.

Later that night, the doorbell rang. 'They're here. Now remember, sweetheart, what do you do for a living?' Silver Shadow asked Blaze Sharp in a tone that conveyed it wasn't a question.

'I write LGBT spy novels under the pen name Blaze Sharp,' Blaze Sharp answered, their shared understanding palpable.

'Good. And what are we not going to tell them?'

Silver asked again, the gravity of the situation evident in her tone.

'That we're actually superspy master assassins,' Blaze replied, a hint of discomfort creeping into her voice.

'Good. And finally, what names are we using?' Silver said, her unease mirroring that of her girlfriend.

'Helen Pilates and Christine Holy,' Blaze said, the use of her former name sending a wave of nausea through her.

'Perfect,' Silver said, opening the door for her parents, Stan and Lucy.

"So this is where you live. Pretty expensive-looking for an author we've never heard of. I trust our little Helen didn't pay for this house all by herself," Stan said angrily.

"Father, for the first and last time, Christine is not a gold digger," Silver Shadow retorted, her tone tinged with stress.

"You still seem stressed. Is she abusing you?" Stan accused.

"Not even romantically or intimately. If anything, I'm the lucky one," Silver explained to her parents.

"Look, don't think like that. I'll find you a new girlfriend who isn't using you for your money and connections," Stan insisted.

"Stan, play nicely. I'm sure this Christine is perfectly nice," Lucy interjected.

"I really am, and I must say, Mrs. Pilates, if Helen looks anything like you when she's your age, I'm the luckiest living lesbian," Blaze Sharp remarked.

"Thank you, Christine. How did your parents react to meeting Helen?" Lucy inquired.

"If that ever happens, I will let you know. They still think I'm at a conversion camp," Blaze said, making Stan and Lucy feel awkward.

"Dinner is ready. I made bacon-wrapped scallops, seafood risotto, beef Wellington, and Baked Alaska for dessert. I also bought three bottles of non-alcoholic wine: one Moscato rosé, one Sauvignon Blanc, and one Cabernet Sauvignon," Blaze announced.

The four of them began to eat and enjoy the meal, engaging in dinner conversation. Suddenly, Blaze heard something outside. She looked out the window and was horrified by what she saw.

"Hey, Helen! Silver!" Blaze exclaimed, finally alerting Silver at the mention of her code name.

"Mom, Dad, both of you, get to the safe room. There's no time to explain," Silver Shadow said urgently, leading her parents to the safe room.

"Helen, what's wrong?" Lucy asked, her worry evident. "Just go," Silver insisted.

"If our little girl is in danger, she will tell us now," Stan ordered, his concern growing.

Blaze Sharp and Silver Shadow shared a quick kiss before Silver continued, "Don't call nine-one-one," to her parents before locking them inside the safe room.

Blaze and Silver extinguished the lights just as the ten commanders broke in.

Blaze Sharp swings a golf club at Commander Love, striking him in the head with force. She then snaps the club in half and impales Commander Love in the heart with the broken pieces. Meanwhile, Silver Shadow grabs a kitchen knife and swiftly slashes at Commander Piety, wiping the blood from the blade on her shirt. She then lunges forward, plunging the knife into Commander Patience and seizing his rifle, unleashing a barrage of gunfire in all directions.

Commander Reticence attempts to tackle Blaze Sharp, but she retaliates by smashing a dinner plate against his face. As Commander Purity advances, Blaze douses him with scalding hot tea, blinding him momentarily before delivering a decisive blow with the teapot.

Spotting Silver in danger, Commander Repose aims his rifle at her, but she swiftly disarms him and turns the weapon on Commander Truth, raining bullets upon him before delivering a fatal kick to Commander Repose's face.

Commander Pacifism tries to subdue Blaze Sharp with a taser, but she swiftly disarms him, incapacitates him with a swift kick to the groin, and snaps his neck with precision.

Meanwhile, Silver Shadow seizes a fire extinguisher, pulls the pin, and unleashes a torrent of foam upon Commander Faith before delivering a fatal blow to his head with the extinguisher.

Not to be outdone, Blaze hurls a sledgehammer at Commander Selflessness, while Silver ensnares him with a shoelace, tightening her grip around his neck until he falls lifeless. Blaze then seizes a pair of scissors, separating them into halves and brutally stabs Commander Selflessness in the eyes with each sharpened edge.

"Are you both alright?" Silver Shadow asked with concern as she opened the door to the safe room.

"Why are you covered in blood? And why are there ten dead people dressed like monks with automatic rifles?" Lucy asked in panic.

"What's going on here? Who are you two?" Stan asked, equally uneasy. Blaze Sharp and Silver Shadow explained everything in detail.

"Next time, tell us sooner," Lucy said, her voice trembling with fear.

"I trust that there are no more secrets," Stan said firmly, his gaze fixed on Blaze. "No, sir," Blaze confirmed.

With the truth revealed, Silver's parents left, processing the shocking turn of events.

"Mr. and Mrs. Pilates, wait, there's actually one more surprise," Blaze said, hurrying after them.

"What is it this time?" Stan inquired, still uncertain about the unfolding events. Blaze Sharp leaned in and whispered the final surprise into their ears.

"Yes, yes, you may," Stan and Lucy agreed, their expressions softening with warmth. "Thank you," Blaze said gratefully as the three of them returned to the main room.

Blaze knelt down, holding Silver's hand with one hand and a ring with the other.

"Silver Shadow, my beloved, will you marry me?" Blaze Sharp's voice trembled with emotion as she proposed to her girlfriend.

"Yes, my darling Blaze Sharp, I will marry you!" Silver's eyes sparkled with joy as she accepted.

CHAPTER FOUR

Despair of Blaze Sharp

"REPEAT AFTER ME, I, BLAZE," Pontius said solemnly, now acting as the minister of Blaze and Silver's wedding.

"I, Blaze," echoed Blaze, her voice filled with euphoria. "Take thee, Silver," Pontius continued.

"Take thee, Silver," Blaze said, her happiness evident in every word. "As my beloved wife," Pontius finished.

"As my beloved wife!" Blaze declared, tears of joy streaming down her cheeks. "Now it's your turn, I, Silver," Pontius prompted.

"I, Silver," said Silver, her heart brimming with delight. "Take thee, Blaze," Pontius continued.

"Take thee, Blaze," Silver echoed, her jubilation

shining through. "As my beloved wife," Pontius finished.

"As my beloved wife!" Silver exclaimed, tears of happiness glistening in her eyes. "As long as you both shall live," Pontius said, sealing the sacred bond.

"We do!" Blaze and Silver affirmed in unison, their voices filled with unwavering commitment.

"I pronounce you two spouses for life. You may kiss your wife," Pontius declared, as the two women leaned in, sealing their vows with a tender kiss, now each other's wives.

"We're under attack! CHURCH soldiers are everywhere!" an Agent shouted, only to be silenced by a fatal shot to the head. Blaze Sharp's heart raced as she reached for her weapons, her gaze meeting Silver's with a shared understanding.

"Silver, my love, shall we have our first dance as wives?" Blaze asked, determination flashing in her eyes.

"If you can read my mind, why do you need to ask?" Silver Shadow giggled, her own weapons at the ready.

In a swift and deadly dance, Blaze hurled three poisoned knives, each finding its mark in the hearts of CHURCH soldiers. Silver spun gracefully, her movements fluid as she decapitated seven assailants with precise strikes.

Blaze executed a precise maneuver, swiftly stabbing a CHURCH soldier in the throat with a deadly pas de bourrée. Meanwhile, Silver deftly wrapped a sash from her wedding dress

around a CHURCH soldier's wrist, guiding his own blade to his jaw, then across his head, with lethal precision.

As the chaos intensified, Blaze improvised, crafting a makeshift molotov cocktail with fireworks and alcohol. With a swift toss, she ignited the concoction, engulfing the room in flames until the sprinklers intervened, shrouding them in a protective veil of steam.

Together, Blaze and Silver fought with a fierce determination, their bond as wives only strengthening their resolve amidst the chaos of battle.

Several weeks later, Silver had a surprise for Blaze. "What is it? I hope it's as amazing as you made it sound," Blaze said, her curiosity piqued.

"Behold our greatest achievement," Silver declared with pride. A holographic image of a non-binary child appeared before them.

"Hello, Mother Blaze. I am Proud Rainbow Intelligence Desiring Equality, but you can call me

PRIDE. I was created by Mother Silver to help both of you when you are in danger," PRIDE announced.

Blaze was overcome with joy at the sight of her child, tears of happiness streaming down her face. There were no words to describe how elated she felt in that moment.

The next week, Blaze and Silver found themselves reluctantly attending a dinner with the seven "virtuous" priests. However, the term "virtuous" was entirely ironic, as each virtue they were named for was contradicted by their actions. Fortunately, Blaze managed to poison all their drinks. Despite this, they remained alive, and chaos erupted in the room as everyone sprung into battle.

Blaze Sharp swiftly hooked her crossbow onto Priest Faith's rifle, yanking it downwards until it pointed vertically. With a deft motion, she pulled the trigger, causing Priest Faith to shoot himself in the foot. In a split second, Blaze shot Priest Faith directly through his eye with her crossbow bolt.

Meanwhile, Silver Shadow engaged Priest Hope, stabbing him in the temple with a bolt, but he remained alive. With a powerful slice of her cutlass sword, Silver sent Priest Hope stumbling into the path of her attack, severing his carotid artery and ending his life.

As Priest Justice brandished an AK-47, Blaze swiftly threw a knife into his hand, pinning it to the trigger. Another knife flew, striking Priest Justice in the aorta, causing him to inadvertently shoot Priest Prudence to death.

Silver targeted Priest Charity with precision shots from her Beretta pistol, AR-15 rifle, HK G3 rifle, MP5K machine gun, and compound bow, systematically incapacitating him before delivering the final blow to his eyes.

Blaze, frustrated by Priest Temperance's stomach-churning antics, swiftly subdued him, tying a noose around his throat and throwing the other end into a wood chipper. She watched with satisfaction as he met his end.

When Priest Fortitude attempted to flee, Blaze immobilized him by slicing his Achilles tendon. With a wicked smile, she and Silver approached, taking the hand grenade from his grasp. Silver, with a seductive grin, planted the grenade on Priest Fortitude, watching with amusement as he panicked and exploded.

Later, during their second honeymoon in Italy, Blaze and Silver were savoring the delicious flavors of timpano and tiramisu. "You don't need to tell me that, dear. We're sharing them," Blaze agreed with a smile.

Suddenly, Silver noticed a red dot aimed at Blaze's heart. Reacting instinctively, she pushed Blaze out of harm's way, taking the hit herself. Blaze, filled with panic, swiftly loaded her crossbow and fired in the direction of the shooter. The bolt struck the sniper's rifle, causing it to explode, but the assailant managed to escape.

"Silver?!" Blaze cried out in despair as she knelt by her beloved's side. "Blaze… I'll always be with you," Silver weakly whispered before succumbing to her wounds.

Back home, Blaze ensured that Silver was laid to rest in a two-person coffin, knowing that they would be reunited in eternity.

CHAPTER FIVE

Quest of Blaze Sharp

BLAZE SHARP HAD BEEN WORKING herself to death trying to find any trace of her wife's killer for almost a year with no luck. Until one day she found exactly what she needed. This was too good to be true but also too good to pass up both she and PRIDE knew that. PRIDE was starting to become concerned for the health, safety and sanity of their last living mother.

However with an opportunity this good nothing could stop Blaze Sharp from avenging her wife. She traveled directly toward the Elbib building next to Eden's menagerie this was the lair of Christian Jesus the leader of CHURCH and the murderer of Silver Shadow!

Blaze Sharp knew she would never make it in and

out of the building alive through the main entrance. Instead she chose to enter the building from the floor that Christian's lair was on from outside the building in the zoological garden. The entrance however was guarded by seven CHURCH soilders.

The seven CHURCH soldiers charged at Blaze Sharp armed with full tang machetes and double action colt revolvers. Blaze Sharp blocked a machete slash from the first soldier stabbing him in the neck with her knife. The second soldier shot at Blaze with his revolver but she deflected the bullet with her knife causing the bullet to land in the third soldier's head killing him. Blaze slashed the second soldier's throat. The fourth one attacked Blaze with an overhead machete chop, Blaze parried the assault throwing her assailant off balance.

Seizing the opportunity Blaze Sharp took action stabbing the fourth soldier in the heart. She grabbed the fifth one's wrist spinning him around and stabbing him in the back. The sixth soldier shot at Blaze with his revolver. Seeing it coming Blaze Sharp grabbed the seventh soldier using him as a human shield. Blaze threw her knife into the sixth soldier's head.

Blaze entered Eden's menagerie continuing her path to justice for her fallen wife.

"Christian, you've certainly set the stage. But now, it's game on!" Blaze Sharp's voice rang out, dripping with competitive fervor that quickly morphed into seething anger. Her eyes scanned the scene before her, taking in the sight of several caged animals being loaded onto an ark destined for the depths of the ocean. A surge of determination coursed through her veins as she vowed not to let such cruelty go unchecked, especially when the chosen victims were known for exhibiting LGBTQ+ behaviors.

With swift and decisive action, Blaze set her plan in motion. Using her skills to pick the lock of a cage filled with New Mexico whiptail lizards, she granted them a chance at freedom just moments before they would meet their watery demise. Yet, her act of defiance did not go unnoticed, drawing the attention of nearby CHURCH soldiers who moved in to intercept her.

A soldier aimed a Glock 18 pistol at Blaze, but she was quicker, disarming him and causing the weapon to discharge, shattering the lock of another cage holding several swans captive. Seizing the opportunity, the liberated birds launched a frenzied attack on the soldiers, creating a diversion that allowed Blaze to slip away.

But her escape was short-lived as another soldier

seized her by the throat, pinning her against a nearby table. Thinking fast, Blaze reached for a handful of hot peppers, crushing them in her grip before grinding them into the soldier's eyes, rendering him temporarily blind.

Using the momentary advantage, she dispatched him with a swift kick, sending him crashing into a cage filled with Japanese Macaques.

Continuing her onslaught, Blaze handcuffed two soldiers together and shoved them face-first into a scorching grill before propelling them into a hyena cage, shattering its door in the process. With her path clear, she ascended a nearby structure just as CHURCH reinforcements arrived in a holycopter, intent on eliminating her.

But Blaze was ready. With precision and determination, she launched a grappling hook around the holycopter's landing gear, swinging toward her target. With impeccable aim, she hurled a poison gas grenade through the small open window of the computer lab below, neutralizing the threat inside.

As the holycopter spiraled out of control, Blaze seized her moment, crashing through a much larger window and landing at the end of a hallway. With the computer lab just two rooms away, she fired her crossbow at the pilot, ensuring the holycopter met its fiery demise on the ground below.

In the midst of the chaos, Blaze's thoughts turned to her beloved Silver. "Don't worry, my love. Soon, you'll finally be at peace," she murmured, her heart heavy with grief yet fueled by a relentless determination to see justice served.

Blaze approached the office of the twelve CHURCH priests, her heart pounding with determination. Jude, one of the priests, emerged from the room clutching a tank labeled "Prism Water," a substance rumored to be the unholiest of all. "Your agency needs this," Jude declared, his voice laden with urgency. "To defeat Christian Jesus, you must synchronize the other tank of this substance to the sprinkler system in his lair. It's the only weakness of Project DEITY, the ultimate weapon of CHURCH." PRIDE, Blaze's trusted companion, confirmed Jude's words as truth.

With a steely resolve, Blaze took matters into her own hands. Sneaking into the office, she swiftly dispatched each of the eleven remaining CHURCH priests with precise shots from her crossbow. Securing the other tank of Prism Water, she knew this was a crucial step in her mission to dismantle CHURCH's power.

Putting her faith in PRIDE's analysis, Blaze followed Jude's instructions to the letter. With the second tank in her possession, she made her way to the computer lab, her mind focused on the next phase of her plan.

As Blaze Sharp stepped into the lab, urgency fueled her every move. With PRIDE's assistance, she swiftly initiated the download of a file crafted by Silver herself—the Crucifixion Virus. This powerful program was designed to obliterate CHURCH's digital infrastructure, wiping out their files, programs, and data. Additionally, it contained a devastating payload: a bomb set to detonate and bring down the entire Elbib building in precisely one hour.

With time ticking away, Blaze wasted no moment. She navigated the labyrinth of digital pathways with precision, her fingers flying over the keyboard as she executed the crucial

download. Each passing second heightened the tension, but Blaze remained focused on the task at hand.

Once the download was underway, Blaze turned her attention to her next objective: confronting Christian in his lair. Guarded by his most formidable soldier monk and skilled medical nun, the path to Christian's sanctum was fraught with danger.

As she approached, the nun's voice cut through the air like a blade. "Well, well, well. Look who dares to venture into the lion's den," she sneered, eyeing Blaze with disdain. Beside her, the monk's gaze narrowed in recognition. "This one seems oddly familiar," he remarked, his tone laced with suspicion.

Blaze froze, disbelief washing over her. "Mother?! Father?!" she exclaimed, her voice trembling with emotion.

In a moment of stunned silence, the truth hung heavy in the air. "Christine?!" they both uttered in disbelief, the weight of their shared past crashing down upon them.

"I no longer answer to that name. You should know me as Blaze Sharp," Blaze declared firmly, her gaze unwavering.

"Christine, what have those sinners done to you?!" Josephine exclaimed, her voice filled with horror and disappointment.

"They've liberated me. They've allowed me to embrace my true self, to find belonging, to understand who I am. All you've ever done is try to mold me into something I'm not. This organization has only brought suffering to my people," Blaze retorted, her words seething with anger and resentment.

"Do you truly believe that?" Marik interjected, genuine curiosity coloring his tone.

"I WITNESS IT EVERY DAY. I have evidence. My wife was murdered by your leader!" Blaze's voice trembled with emotion, her pain raw and palpable. Her words shocked Marik and filled Josephine with disgust.

"You married a woman! You're in need of salvation now more than ever!" Josephine's words were sharp, her tone accusatory.

"No, it's you who requires salvation," Blaze shot back, her voice steady and resolute.

"That's enough! If she cannot be saved, then she must be eradicated! Marik, eliminate her!" Josephine's command echoed through the room as Marik unsheathed his flaming broadsword, launching himself at Blaze with fiery determination.

With swift precision, Blaze deftly countered Marik's attacks, using only her knife to thwart his advances and disarm him. In a surprising display of mercy, she spared her father's life.

"I'm going in there. I'm taking down Christian and seeking justice for my beloved Silver," Blaze declared, her resolve unshakable.

"Never!" Josephine roared, her anger boiling over

as she pulled a lever, triggering a trapdoor beneath Blaze's feet. With a sudden lurch, Blaze plummeted into a den of mechanical lions, her fate hanging in the balance.

Blaze Sharp effortlessly subdued the mechanical lions, using the last one as a springboard to propel herself to safety. Snatching up the flaming broadsword, she swiftly disarmed Josephine with a well-aimed strike from the hilt, rendering her unconscious.

"PRIDE, kindly escort these two to the agency as prisoners," Blaze commanded with a tone of authority and courtesy. Without hesitation, PRIDE complied, guiding Josephine and Marik away while Blaze turned her attention to the room where justice awaited for her beloved Silver.

CHAPTER SIX

Battle of Blaze Sharp

BLAZE SHARP CONFRONTED the man responsible for her wife's death, her gaze unyielding as she met his sinister smirk. "We finally meet, Blaze Sharp, or may I call you Christine?" Christian taunted, his voice dripping with malice.

"No, you may not," Blaze retorted, her tone laced with venomous anger.

Christian chuckled darkly, relishing in his taunts. "You should know, my plan was to kill you, not the sinner you married," he admitted, his laughter echoing through the room.

"You're a monster!" Blaze seethed, her fingers tightening around the grip of her crossbow, poised to strike.

With a malicious grin, Christian unleashed a

blinding burst of light, disrupting Blaze's aim. "If you dare challenge a god, you should prepare to face your reckoning, Blaze," he sneered.

Blaze met his challenge with unwavering resolve. "There's no such thing as a god, so let's end this," she declared, her voice resolute and defiant.

"Thou shalt receive judgment by thunder!" Christian's voice boomed, summoning lightning strikes to assault Blaze.

"Who do I look like, Ben Franklin?" Blaze retorted, her movements swift as she evaded the electrifying onslaught.

"Clearly, you need to spend some time in my garden!" Christian bellowed, conjuring sentient plants that lunged at Blaze with ferocity.

With a deft motion, Blaze wielded the flaming broadsword, cutting through the vines that ensnared her. "Sorry, but I don't have much of a green thumb," she quipped, her tone laced with sarcasm.

"With a name like Blaze, you must like fire!" Christian's frustration grew evident as he summoned fireballs to rain down upon Blaze.

Blaze remained composed amidst the fiery onslaught. "There are worse things than a little fire," she remarked, her demeanor unwavering.

"I'll wash you away with a flood!" Christian's

anger intensified, filling the room with crashing waves.

"I know how to swim," Blaze responded calmly, her resolve unshaken.

"You LGBT spies are a plague of snakes!" Christian's rage reached its peak as he unleashed a horde of serpents to assail Blaze.

Blaze Sharp swiftly dispatched the millions of serpents that Christian had unleashed, her resolve unyielding. "Is that all you've got? I expected more from a so-called deity," she chuckled, her voice laced with defiance.

"I still have one last trick up my sleeve!" Christian erupted with fury, his eyes blazing with malice. Blaze Sharp's heart skipped a beat as she watched her beloved wife, Silver Shadow, rise from the dead. Overwhelmed with emotion, Blaze rushed forward and enveloped Silver in a tight embrace. "Silver, my love! I thought I would never see you again," Blaze cried, her voice trembling with a mixture of joy and relief. She was about to say more when something unexpected occurred.

Blaze Sharp was suddenly engulfed in searing agony, a sharp pain piercing her torso, causing her to release her beloved Silver Shadow from their embrace.

As she looked down, her heart shattered to see that it was Silver who had fired the shot.

"Silver, my love, why?" Blaze cried out, her voice filled with despair and disbelief.

"She's not your love anymore. Now she's a mindless killing machine, as powerful as you are. Best of all, she only obeys me!" Christian's laughter echoed through the chamber, a chilling sound that sent shivers down Blaze's spine.

"You fiend!" Blaze rasped, her words laced with agony as she struggled to comprehend the betrayal unfolding before her.

Marionette Silver lunged at Blaze with relentless ferocity, her attacks relentless and unforgiving. Despite the pain and anguish coursing through her, Blaze refused to retaliate, unwilling to harm the one she loved. With each blow, Blaze's injuries mounted, while Silver remained untouched—a cruel testament to the purity of Blaze's love, too sacred to endanger Silver's well-being.

Meanwhile, back at the Lethal Government Battle Tactics agency, Christian's nefarious use of Project DEITY plunged the once-secure facility into chaos. The water coursing through the agency's plumbing twisted into a grotesque red, resembling blood—a chilling omen of the horrors to come.

A relentless horde of toxic frogs surged through the halls, their croaks echoing ominously as they spread chaos and panic among the agents. Simultaneously, a plague of lice infested every agent, spreading discomfort and distraction with each relentless bite.

As if summoned by malevolent forces, swarms of flies descended upon the agency, their buzzing wings heralding the onset of further turmoil. Agents, already beleaguered by the onslaught of afflictions, found themselves stricken with sudden and severe cases of acne, adding insult to injury.

Then, as if nature itself had turned against them, an indoor hailstorm pummeled the building, shattering windows and wreaking havoc on the interior. The relentless assault continued as a locust plague descended upon the agency, devouring everything in its path and leaving devastation in its wake.

In the midst of the chaos, darkness descended as the agency suffered a crippling blackout, plunging the once-bustling facility into a realm of shadow and uncertainty.

Just when all seemed lost, a figure emerged—a deathly omen known as the Death Legna, poised to claim the souls of every agent within its grasp. Yet, in a twist of fate, the calamities that had beset the agency suddenly transformed, turning to stone or dust, while the agents themselves were miraculously healed, their spirits undaunted in the face of adversity.

Blaze Sharp teetered on the edge of oblivion, locked in a deadly dance with a

puppeteer-controlled apparition of her deceased wife. Christian's malicious laughter echoed through the room, taunting her with the cruel twist of fate that had befallen them both.

As Blaze's strength waned and darkness threatened to claim her, a urgent voice pierced through the chaos. "Mother Blaze, activate the prism water now!" PRIDE's urgent directive cut through the haze of despair, injecting a surge of hope into Blaze's heart.

With a swift motion, Blaze raised her crossbow and aimed at the sprinkler system, unleashing a torrent of prism water that cascaded over the room like a cleansing tide. In an instant, the healing properties of the water enveloped her, restoring her to full strength, while the marionette Silver was frozen in place, then disintegrated into dust.

Tears welled in Blaze's eyes as she watched her beloved perish once again before her eyes. But there was no time for grief, no space for remorse. PRIDE, ever vigilant, seized control of the technology, ensnaring Christian Jesus in a web of wires, binding him in a crucifix position.

"This is for myself," Blaze declared, her voice a thunderous roar as she unleashed a barrage of crossbow bolts, each one a testament to her righteous fury. One pierced through his right hand, another through his left, and a third through his feet, marking each grievance he had inflicted upon her and her people.

With steely resolve, Blaze retrieved her knife, its gleaming edge reflecting the fire of her determination. "This is for Silver Shadow!" she spat, hurling the blade with unerring precision, its trajectory ending in a final, fatal blow as it pierced through Christian's eyes.

Without a backward glance, Blaze exited the Elbib building, leaving behind the wreckage of her vengeance. She walked away, her steps unyielding, her resolve unbroken. And as she crossed the threshold, the building erupted in a cataclysmic explosion, leaving nothing but a smoldering crater—a testament to the justice she had wrought.

CHAPTER SEVEN

Ghost of Blaze Sharp

BLAZE SHARP strode back into the LGBT agency, greeted by cheers and accolades from her comrades. "There she is, our heroine!" Sorceress exclaimed with a grin.

"You'll be pleased to know that former priest Jude has switched sides and joined the agency as the leader of our newest branch, the straight allies," Pontius informed her with a proud smile.

Blaze nodded appreciatively. "That's great news. Anything else I should be aware of?"

"We've already recruited several new agents for the straight allies branch. Why don't you take a moment to introduce yourself?" Pontius suggested.

Blaze mingled with the new recruits, recognizing some familiar faces among them. There were Silver's parents, Zelda Black—her childhood friend and former crush—and even Marik, her own father.

"What about Josephine?" Blaze inquired, her tone betraying her disdain.

Marik sighed, clearly exasperated by the mention of his ex. "That bigot is still in her cell, refusing to learn from the deconversion therapy."

Blaze's lips curled in a sardonic smile. "Well, I guess I'll have a chat with her myself." Making her way to the holding cells, Blaze entered Josephine's confinement.

"Nice to see you again," she greeted, the sarcasm dripping from her words.

"Christine, you should know your father and I are divorced because he chose to side with those sinners you seem to like so much," Josephine remarked with disappointment.

"Lucky him," Blaze retorted, cutting off her mother's attempt at conversation. "Christine—"

"Let me stop you right there. My name is Blaze. You can call me by that name or not at all," Blaze interrupted, her tone firm and unwavering.

"Listen, young lady. Why don't you ditch these sinners and come with me to the heavenly kingdom?

Just you and me. Doesn't that sound like the dream, Christine?" Josephine pleaded.

A single tear traced its path down Blaze's cheek, not out of regret for what she was about to do, but for the fact that she hadn't done it years ago.

"Enjoy your time there… without me," Blaze declared, her voice calm yet resolute, before delivering a fatal blow to the woman who had once been her mother.

As she left the cell, Blaze couldn't shake the feeling of melancholy that washed over her. It wasn't because she had taken a life, but because that life had never truly been her mother's. The woman she had just killed had only ever wanted Christine Holy—someone Blaze Sharp could never be.

Shortly thereafter, Blaze Sharp delivered some jarring news to her superiors. "You're resigning? But you're indispensable! You single handedly dismantled CHURCH!" Sorceress and Pontius exclaimed, their shock palpable as they grappled with the idea of losing not only their top agent but also a dear friend.

"I'm not leaving you empty-handed. My replacement surpasses me in every aspect," Blaze assured them, though her words left them baffled, as if she had just proclaimed the impossible—a notion that seemed increasingly plausible as they looked upon the enigmatic figure she presented.

"And who might this replacement be?" they inquired, skepticism coloring their tone. "Right here," Blaze replied, placing PRIDE atop Pontius' desk. "PRIDE is ready for

autonomy, and with this," she added, sliding a flash drive next to PRIDE, "we can enhance their capabilities."

Pontius examined the flash drive with curiosity. "What's on this?"

"I acquired the plans for Project DEITY and made significant enhancements. Allow me to introduce Project RAINBOW—Righteous Atheist Individual Never Bigoting Our Ways," Blaze announced proudly.

"They're impeccable. Thank you, Blaze. However, we can't let you depart without a severance package. So, instead of resigning, consider yourself terminated," Pontius declared, extending a gesture of goodwill to his departing agent.

"Thank you. It's difficult to bid farewell to this place, but I no longer require it," Blaze said tearfully, her emotions a mix of sorrow and relief as she left the agency behind.

Unbeknownst to her colleagues, Blaze was

haunted by dreams of Silver's ghost visiting her every night, while she faithfully visited Silver's grave each day. Eventually, on the anniversary of Silver's passing, Blaze succumbed to broken heart syndrome. Their spirits were interred together in a shared coffin, where they found solace in each other's embrace, even in death.

Meanwhile, PRIDE rapidly ascended to become the agency's preeminent member.

Composed of pridium and empowered by Project RAINBOW, PRIDE emerged as a

near-omnipotent and virtually indestructible force, ensuring the legacy of Blaze and Silver lived on in their own unique way.

CHAPTER EIGHT

Renewal of Blaze Sharp

AMIDST THE DESOLATION of the Elbib building's ruins, an unforeseen power lay dormant within Project DEITY, unbeknownst to Blaze Sharp. This power was reincarnation, which granted Christian Jesus the ability to rise from the ashes of death. With his resurrection, he forged his most formidable weapon yet—the Thorn Halo. Infused with the dark arts of necromancy, the Thorn Halo bestowed upon him the ability to command an army of worshiper zombies bound solely to his will.

"Now, my children, spread your prayers like wildfire," Christian cackled, his voice echoing through the shattered halls. The zombies heeded his call, dispersing across the land, chanting a sinister litany in unison.

"Our master, take us to heaven, so we may chant your name, your kingdom comes, beyond the dead, your slaves we'll be in heaven, for every day, we give you bread, no sinner will ever trespass, and we forgive you for trespassing in our lives, we allow your manipulation, because free will is evil, our honour as servants, for our master, forever and ever, amen,"the zombies intoned ceaselessly, their voices a haunting chorus that echoed through the ages.

Two men sat across from each other, their blind date unfolding in unexpected ways. One, a member of the agency, carried secrets beneath a veneer of normalcy. The other, a civilian, had yet to grasp the extraordinary world he was about to encounter.

As they conversed, the civilian's attention was drawn to a peculiar figure—someone praying fervently and striding into oncoming traffic. Reacting swiftly, the civilian lunged forward, pushing the stranger out of harm's way. "Are you alright? What were you thinking?" he inquired, only to find his hands involuntarily clasped in a prayer position by the stranger.

Instantly, the civilian found himself chanting the same cryptic prayer, his mind clouded by a force beyond his comprehension. Meanwhile, the agency member observed this strange phenomenon unfolding, recognizing the telltale signs of danger. With growing alarm, he realized that others were succumbing to the same mysterious influence, transforming into mindless zombies.

Drawing on his training, the agent acted decisively, dispatching a nearby zombie with a swift blow to the head. Racing to the nearest entrance of the agency, he activated the emergency protocols, alerting PRIDE to the dire situation unfolding outside.

"Mayday, mayday, emergency!" he exclaimed urgently, his voice tinged with urgency. "What's happening?" PRIDE responded, concern evident in their digital voice.

"Threat level Christian!" the agent declared, his words laden with gravity. "But that's impossible, he's dead," PRIDE countered, struggling to comprehend the severity of the situation.

In response, the agent swiftly accessed surveillance feeds, revealing the grim reality to his colleagues. The world outside teemed with worshiper zombies, their twisted devotion heralding a threat unlike any they had faced before.

"I have a plan," PRIDE announced, producing two test tubes containing DNA samples—one from Blaze and the other from Silver—and two USB drives labeled accordingly. "Activate the cloning machines," they ordered without hesitation.

"But PRIDE, are you certain? This could be risky, and we have only one opportunity," the agent interjected, voicing valid concerns.

"This is not up for debate. It's an order," PRIDE insisted sternly. "The only ones equipped to handle this are myself and my mothers. Now, bring them back!"

With a sense of urgency, the agents initiated the cloning process. Hours passed with tense anticipation until, finally, the clones of Blaze Sharp and Silver Shadow opened their eyes, returning to life after a decade of absence. It was a moment filled with both relief and uncertainty, marking the beginning of a new chapter fraught with possibilities and challenges.

CHAPTER NINE

Treason of Blaze Sharp

BLAZE, Silver, and PRIDE prepared themselves for battle, ensuring they were armed to the teeth with an array of powerful equipment. Each of them was equipped with one of PRIDE's ingenious inventions. Blaze carried the Allywatch, a multifunctional device capable of summoning tools, gadgets, and weapons to aid her in combat. It boasted an impressive array of features including recording devices, cameras, lie detectors, communication tools, radar, night vision, thermal imaging, sound amplifiers, sonar, black lights, magnets, hacking capabilities, scanners, and more. Ironically, the only thing it couldn't do was tell time.

Silver wielded a potent potion known as Project Samson, stolen from the remnants of CHURCH. This potion bestowed upon her the strength of millions, amplifying her combat abilities to extraordinary levels.

PRIDE, in their upgraded battle mode, sported formidable enhancements including meter-long scalpel-sharp claw blades, rocket-powered wings that launched razor-sharp boomerang blades, a plasma gun, a thundergun, an acid sprayer, a six-barrel speargun

capable of firing spears individually or simultaneously, a sun cannon, and numerous other deadly armaments.

Before stepping onto the battlefield, Blaze affectionately embraced Silver, sharing a passionate French kiss as a final display of their love and solidarity.

Blaze, Silver, and PRIDE waged a relentless onslaught against the zombie horde, dispatching them with ruthless efficiency. Blaze conjured an arsenal of weapons, ranging from blades and bludgeons to firearms and explosives, leaving no undead creature unscathed. Meanwhile, Silver's newfound strength enabled her to pulverize zombies with her bare fists, effortlessly crushing their ranks.

PRIDE, in their formidable battle form, proved to be an unstoppable force against the zombie menace, tearing through their ranks with ruthless precision. Despite their combined might, the trio faced a critical vulnerability within their midst.

As the battle raged on, Blaze found herself succumbing to the overwhelming onslaught of the undead, her strength waning. Recognizing the dire situation, her family was forced to make a heartbreaking decision. Reluctantly, they were compelled to leave Blaze behind, a decision that weighed heavily on their hearts as they departed, their resolve tested like never before.

Midst the grief over Blaze's apparent loss, Silver and PRIDE received a distressing call from Pontius. "Silver, I have unsettling news. We received a message from Blaze, but it's… peculiar," Pontius relayed before playing the recorded mantra. "I condemn you to an eternal slumber, a creep without number, your life I'll forsake before dawn's light, your fate sealed tight," echoed the eerie voice of the zombie Blaze.

Immediately, Silver and PRIDE were whisked away to Christian's presumed whereabouts. There, to their horror, they found him caressing Blaze's head as if she were his pet. "Release

her, you monster!" Silver's voice reverberated with a chilling intensity, enough to give even the most hardened criminals pause. Yet, Christian merely chuckled at the reaction.

"Why would I do that? She's under my control now, and it's time for her to cleanse her sins. Christine, rid the world of that temptress," Christian jeered, commanding the zombie Blaze to act.

Without a hint of emotion, zombie Blaze obeyed, summoning an AK-47 and firing at Silver, who collapsed lifeless to the ground, blood staining her shirt. "Now, eliminate that abomination," Christian urged, as zombie Blaze aimed a harpoon gun at PRIDE, narrowly missing.

"You missed!" Christian seethed in frustration. Yet, with a cunning smile, zombie Blaze retorted, "Did I?" The harpoon ricocheted, shattering the thorn halo in a dramatic revelation.

As the truth unfolded, Blaze emerged unscathed, and Silver revealed she was never harmed. "PRIDE, let justice rain," Blaze commanded solemnly. PRIDE unleashed a torrent of prism water, engulfing Christian and reducing him to vapor in an instant.

Returning to the agency, Blaze disclosed her ingenious plan—she had discreetly filled Silver's bra with blood bags, tricking Christian into believing his deception had succeeded, a feat she deemed the most challenging she had ever faced.

CHAPTER TEN

Power of Blaze Sharp

BLAZE SHARP FACED YET another trial, one deemed impossible by many. "I am the Godly Omnipotent Deity. Bring forth the one known as Blaze Sharp!" boomed a creature of immense size and power. Unfazed, Blaze stepped forward to confront this imposing being. "I stand before you," she declared, defiant and resolute.

"When I vanquish you, all shall forsake their sinful paths and embrace the ways of CHURCH!" declared GOD, laying down the terms of their confrontation.

"On two conditions: first, as long as I draw breath, they shall be shielded from harm; second, if I emerge victorious, love shall never again be deemed sinful," Blaze Sharp countered, firm in her resolve.

"It is agreed!" proclaimed GOD, before summoning nine fearsome beasts known as legnas to do battle. Blaze fought valiantly against the legnas, seeming on the verge of triumph. Yet, GOD grew weary of the contest and decided to intervene personally, intent on striking Blaze down himself.

Blaze Sharp awoke, finding herself standing atop a frozen lake of ice. Before her stood a tenth legna, frozen from the waist down, its size and power rivaled only by the Godly Omnipotent Deity itself. "Is this the underworld? Are you the anti-GOD?" Blaze inquired, her voice echoing across the icy expanse.

"I am known by many names, but Damien is my preferred one," the anti-GOD replied solemnly.

"What transgression led you to be banished here?" Blaze inquired, curious about Damien's plight.

"I sought to grant humanity a choice, to embrace free will. For that, I was condemned," Damien explained, his voice tinged with sorrow.

"It's unjust. You were punished for seeking something noble," Blaze remarked, her empathy evident.

"You're the first to truly understand my plight," Damien confessed, tears of lava streaming down his face.

"We may find solace here, but I'm bound to leave soon, never to return," Blaze lamented.

"Indeed, but before you depart, there are those who wish to speak with you. Once they're done, you shall depart with all my powers, to be reclaimed upon your return," Damien proposed, striking a deal with Blaze. And so, one by one, familiar faces began to appear, each with words to share with Blaze Sharp.

The first to address Blaze was former priest Jude. "I joined your side because I believe in its right-eousness. You'll prove to me it's also the winning side," he declared before fading away,

making room for Zelda Black. "No one dictates who Blaze Sharp can or cannot be. This creature doesn't know a thing about you," she asserted before giving way to Sorceress Fiend. "You're not just the best in our branch, but the finest this agency has ever known. Show this beast that Blaze Sharp is unbreak-able," she urged before Prime Minister Pontius took her place. "I recruited you because I saw your poten-tial. Now is the time to prove me right," he stated firmly before Marik stepped forward. "I'm here to meet my true daughter, the one named Blaze Sharp," he declared before fading, replaced by Josephine. "You resist my conversion, yet you yield to GOD. How laughable," she sneered before vanishing, leaving Christian Jesus in her wake. "You've killed me twice, only to meet your end by my father's hand. I expected better," he taunted before disappearing, making way for PRIDE. "I believe in your victory, not just through calculations, but because of something more human," they affirmed before Silver Shadow appeared. "That monster fights out of ignorance, but you fight for love. Is our love true? Is it pure? Prove to that monster that it's unbreakable," she implored before fading away, leaving Blaze to return to Earth, her size and power matching that of GOD. Adorned with rainbow horns, bat wings, and wielding a spear of rainbow hues, Blaze stood ready for the ultimate battle.

Empowered as Legna Blaze Sharp, she swiftly dispatched the nine legnas before confronting the GOD. Armed with her spear, Legna Blaze Sharp clashed with the GOD, who wielded a flaming broadsword of equal magnitude. Their battle raged on until the GOD, for the first time, appeared vulnerable to mortality.

"All I sought was to guide humanity toward its best path," the GOD lamented.

"We prefer forging our own destinies," Legna Blaze Sharp retorted before delivering a fatal blow, piercing the GOD's heart with her spear. The GOD perished in agony, descending into the underworld.

As the power left her, Blaze Sharp reverted to her

Conclusion

We now come to the end of this book, but the beginning of a new chapter for you. I hope that you have participated in each chapter of this book and the only thing left now is for you to take action. If you did not participate while reading, I suggest you go back and start the process as outlined in these chapters.

Don't let your life pass you by. Create the life you want, for only you can do that. This book is but one resource. Never stop developing yourself and remember, you need to continuously develop yourself. Your body can't live on yesterday's or last week's food and it is the same with your inner growth. You need to continuously feed your mind. Remember what I quoted in an earlier chapter: *If you don't maintain something, it will deteriorate.*

I want to share another quotation from Zig Ziglar: *People often say that motivation doesn't last. Well, neither does bathing – that's why we recommend it daily.*

I want to remind you of what I suggested to you in the introduction of this book. I provided you with a definition for success. I made a suggestion that you read this book to the end and then, when you have completed the book, come back to the definition and read it again. Let me expand on this request. If you have participated in the process outlined in this book up to the chapter that deals with planning, and you have completed the process, I want you to read the definition again. Let me share the definition again with you:

My definition of success is as follows: *Achieving a goal you have purposefully planned for. By achieving this goal, you enhance your life's purpose and contribute to a better life for you and those around you.*

Let me reiterate what I have said: if you have followed through on each of the steps in this book up to the planning chapter, which is very straightforward, you should be able to relate to the definition in a more purposeful way, because you should be able to measure your progress and determine whether you are succeeding or not. When reading this definition, then, it should have more meaning and purpose for you, coupled with a clear direction that you can relate to and derive benefit from that makes this definition real to you. It will be different to when you read it the first time.

> *The only impossible journey is the one you never begin.*
> **Tony Robbins**

I want to encourage you to enjoy the ride and share this book with someone else. Go out there, and succeed anyway! I want to end this book with a poem by Edgar Guest which is titled:

Don't Quit
Edgar Guest

When things go wrong, as they sometimes will,
When the road you're trudging seems all up hill,
When the funds are low and the debts are high,
And you want to smile, but you have to sigh,
When care is pressing you down a bit,
Rest if you must – but don't you quit.

Life is queer, with its twists and turns,
As every one of us sometimes learns,
And many a failure turns about
When he might have won had he stuck it out;
Don't give up, though the pace seems slow –
You may succeed with another blow.

Often the goal is nearer than
It seems to a faint and faltering man,
Often the struggler has given up
When he might have captured the victor's cup,
And he learned too late, when the night slipped down,
How close he was to the golden crown.

Success is failure turned inside out –
The silver tint of the clouds of doubt,
And you never can tell how close you are,
It may be near when it seems afar;
So stick to the fight when you're hardest hit –
It's when things seem worst that you mustn't quit.

normal self, no longer needing the divine strength. Subsequently, a peace agreement was reached between the LGBT agency and CHURCH, recognizing the validity of love in all its forms. With this, Blaze, Silver, and PRIDE could enjoy a lifetime of happiness together.

THE END.

www.ingramcontent.com/pod-product-compliance
Lightning Source LLC
Chambersburg PA
CBHW061432050726
47593CB00006B/2324